SHALOM CIAO HOLA

OLA YO KONICHIWA

WOOF AL SALAAM A'ALAYKUM

JAMBO NI HAO CIAO JAMBO

LAYKUM HOLA BONJOUR

SHALOM KONICHIWA

BONJOUR HELLO WOOF NI HAO

YO

AL SALAAM A'ALAYKUM CIAO

BONJOUR SHALOM

YO

OOF JAMBO NI HAO HELLO

AL SALAAM A'ALAYKUM

Say HELLO!

Rachel Isadora

G. P. Putnam's Sons • An Imprint of Penguin Group (USA) Inc.

G. P. PUTNAM'S SONS
A division of Penguin Young Readers Group.
Published by The Penguin Group.
Penguin Group (USA) Inc., 375 Hudson Street, New York, NY 10014, U.S.A.
Penguin Group (Canada), 90 Eglinton Avenue East, Suite 700, Toronto, Ontario M4P 2Y3, Canada (a division of Pearson Penguin Canada Inc.).
Penguin Books Ltd, 80 Strand, London WC2R 0RL, England.
Penguin Ireland, 25 St. Stephen's Green, Dublin 2, Ireland (a division of Penguin Books Ltd.).
Penguin Group (Australia), 250 Camberwell Road, Camberwell, Victoria 3124, Australia (a division of Pearson Australia Group Pty Ltd).
Penguin Books India Pvt Ltd, 11 Community Centre, Panchsheel Park, New Delhi - 110 017, India.
Penguin Group (NZ), 67 Apollo Drive, Rosedale, North Shore 0632, New Zealand (a division of Pearson New Zealand Ltd).
Penguin Books (South Africa) (Pty) Ltd, 24 Sturdee Avenue, Rosebank, Johannesburg 2196, South Africa.
Penguin Books Ltd, Registered Offices: 80 Strand, London WC2R 0RL, England.

Published simultaneously in Canada.
Manufactured in China by RR Donnelley Asia Printing Solutions Ltd.
Design by Marikka Tamura.
Text set in P22JohnstonUnderground.
The illustrations were done with oil paints, printed paper and palette paper.
Library of Congress Cataloging-in-Publication Data
Isadora, Rachel.
Say hello! / Rachel Isadora. p. cm.
Summary: A little girl greets people in her neighborhood in many different languages.
[1. Language and languages—Fiction. 2. Salutations—Fiction. 3. Neighborhood—Fiction. 4. City and town life—Fiction.] I. Title.
PZ7.I763Say 2010 [E]—dc22 2009011318
ISBN 978-0-399-25230-3
1 1

Hello . . .

Nancy, Cecilia, Marikka, Zelda, Sara,
Nora, Ronni, Kathy, Franca, Jill, Ed, Caryn,
Barbara, Lou, Catherine, Abe, Marci, Cindy, Larry,
ML, Alan, Amy, Steven, Jen, Ron, Mitch, Jenny, Hiram,
Gary, Maria, Claire, Lori, Bruce, Richard, Elizabeth, Fred,
Janet, Andrew, Rebecca, James, David, Laura,
Millie, Joe, Evan . . . and Uncle Hy

Carmelita gets up early in the morning.

She helps her mama make their favorite breakfast, huevos con tocino.

"Today we visit Abuela Rosa," Mama says.

12
9
3
6

After breakfast, Carmelita hurries and gets dressed . . . then gets Manny.

BODEGA
Bienvenidos
HABICHUELAS
PICO DE GALLO
Preparamos Comida para toda Ocasión
POLLO
ARROZ
ENSALADAS
CERDO
PLATOS MEXICANOS

They walk all the way down Ninth Avenue.
"Buenos días!" Señor Enrico calls.

"Shalom!" says Mrs. Rosen
and her children.
SHALOM!
WOOF!

Shalom!

They stop in at the Japanese
restaurant to say hello.
Konichiwa!
KONICHIWA!
WOOF!

Osaka

Down the street, they meet Joseph and his parents, who have just come back from Kenya.

Jambo!

Town
CLEANERS
$5.95
SHIRTS
BOX
1396
$6.95
Ring, We Bring
FREE DELIVERY

They pass by a bakery. Carmelita stops to look in the window.

"Let's go in to get some cookies," her mama says.

BONJOUR!
WOOF!

Bonjour!
"Your dog speaks French too!" the woman says, smiling.
WOOF!

Halal Butcher
AL SALAAM A'ALAYKUM!
Al salaam a'alaykum!
WOOF!

meat
eggs

PIZZA
CALZONES
PIZZA
Ciao!
CIAO!
STROMBOLINI
SPAGHETTI
LASAGNA
BAKED MANICOTTI
DRINKS
TAKE OUT
FAST FREE DELIVERY
WOOF!
SALADS

3351
NI HAO!
Ni hao!
NO PARKING DOCTORS ONLY
WOOF!

In the park, Carmelita meets her friends Max and Angel.

"You're one smart snoop dawg," Angel says.

NO PARKING
YIELD
NO PARKING ON GRASS OR SIDEWALK

When they turn the corner, Abuela Rosa is waiting for them.

HOLA!

Hola!
WOOF!

"Manny seems to know what I'm saying," Abuela Rosa says with a wink.

"Manny knows how to say hello in many languages," Carmelita says, smiling.

JINGLE!

JINGLE!

"It's the ice cream truck!"
Abuela Rosa says.

ICE CREAM

WOOF!

"That means Manny wants some too!" Carmelita says, and gives Manny a big hug.

These are the **HELLOS** you'll find in this book:

AL SALAAM A' ALAYKUM Ahl sah-LAHM ah ah-LAY-koom Arabic

BONJOUR Bohn-ZHOOR French

BUENOS DIAS BWE-nos DEE-ahs Spanish

CIAO CHOW Italian

HOLA OH-la Spanish

JAMBO JAM-bo Swahili

KONICHIWA (also **KONNICHIWA**) Koh-NEE-chee-wah Japanese

NI HAO Nee how Mandarin (Chinese)

SHALOM sha-LOHM Hebrew

BONJOUR YO HELLO

NI HAO KONICHIWA HO

CIAO

AL SALAAM A'ALAYKUM

JAMBO WOOF NI HAO

HOLA CIAO SHALOM

AL SALAAM A

WOOF HELL

BONJOUR

AL SALAAM A'ALAYKUM JAMBO

YO KONICHIWA CIAO

HELLO NI HAO HOL

KONICHIWA SHALOM

WOOF BONJOUR YO